To..

"You are wonderfully made,
I hope you enjoy reading
my story.

From Max"

For Ariana, Kaitlin, Samuel and Emma: "Dream big"

"Do not look on his appearance or on the height of his stature...for God sees not as man sees: man looks on the outward appearance but God looks on the heart" (1 Samuel 16:7, The Bible ESV)

"I can do all things through Christ who strengthens me"
(Phillipians 4:13, The Bible)

Matador
9 Priory Business Park,
Wistow Road, Kibworth Beauchamp,
Leicestershire. LE8 0RX
Tel: 0116 279 2299
Email: books@troubador.co.uk
Web: www.troubador.co.uk/matador
Twitter: @matadorbooks

ISBN 978 1785890 468

British Library Cataloguing in Publication Data.
A catalogue record for this book is available from the British Library.

happydesigner
© Illustration and Design by Sarah-Leigh Wills.
www.happydesigner.co.uk

Matador is an imprint of Troubador Publishing Ltd

Strong and Mighty Max

Written by
Kristina Gray

Illustrated by
Sarah-Leigh Wills

I am strong and my heart is big.

My name is Max and I love superheroes.

My favourite ones can fly in the sky.
They can climb the highest mountains
and swim in the deepest of seas.

I play superheroes all the time.
I am strong, see my muscles? I am
mighty and dream the biggest dreams.

I can ride my bike super fast. I have the
best of friends. They are like me, they love
superheroes too.

When I was born the doctor told my mummy and daddy that I have achondroplasia.

This is a big word, it is not a special superpower it just means that my bones grow differently.

I have three sisters. They were not born with achondroplasia. We are all born different.

Some of us have brown eyes, some of us have blue eyes. Some of us have dark skin and some of us have light skin. Some of us are loud and bold like a lion, whilst others are quiet and timid like mice.

My older sisters are twins. They are not identical so they look different.

My baby sister is younger than me, and probably one day she will be taller than me. I will still be her big brother because I am older than she is. I love being her big brother. She's a baby and I am a boy.

Achondroplasia makes my arms and legs shorter. I am smaller than lots of my friends.

My hands are different too. I have amazing hands. My fingers can stretch really far apart and I can make my hand look like a starfish. Can you do that?

What special thing can you do?
We are all amazing in different ways.

My sisters and I love gymnastics and dancing together. I have the best break dancing moves and can spin really fast on my tummy.

My favourite gymnastics position is when I lift my legs high in the sky. My legs bend super-high above my head. When I close my eyes I imagine I can fly.

Each day I grow stronger.

I am not the tallest superhero but I am one of the strongest. I can do most things but sometimes I need to be creative and do things differently.

When I am older, I could be an engineer and design the coolest car, or be a pilot and fly around the world. That would be epic! Or I could be a doctor and help people who are sick.

I also like the idea of putting out fires and catching baddies, so maybe I'll be a fireman or policeman. I wonder what job I will do when I become an adult?

There are so many things that I can be.

My heart is big, my dreams are bigger, and my life will always be a great adventure.

You can call me Strong and Mighty Max.

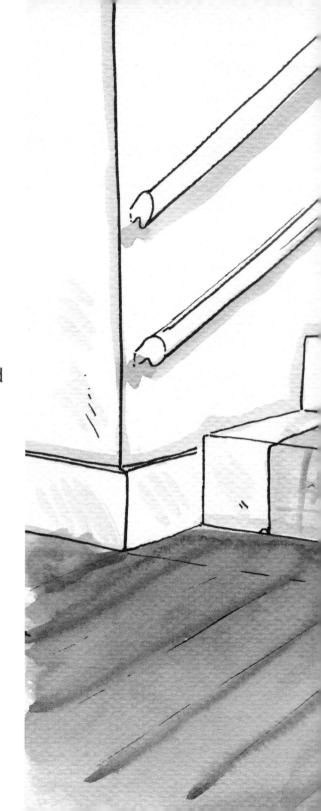

In life you can do all things when strengthened by a greater power.

God is the biggest power of all and he has chosen me to be part of his family. Not because I am tall, not because I am small, but because he loves me and most of all he loves my big heart.

I am Strong and Mighty Max.

About Achondroplasia

*There are over 200 different types of dwarfism and achondroplasia (pronounced ay-kon-dro-play-zha) is the most common type. Approximately 1 in 25,000 babies in the UK will be born with achondroplasia

*It is a genetic condition in which a person is of very short stature because of restricted growth of bones and cartilage. Some conditions which cause restricted growth affect the whole body equally, but the growth of a person with achondroplasia is 'disproportionate' (i.e. unequal) because growth is most restricted in the long bones of the legs and arms, while the trunk is near to average size. The average height for an adult with achondroplasia is between 1m 12 and 1m 45 (approx. 3'8" to 4'9").

*A person born with achondroplasia has normal intelligence, some people wrongly assume that a small body means a small brain, but people with achondroplasia have the same range of intelligence as the general population.*The majority of children born with achondroplasia have no previous family history of the condition, in fact 80% of children are born to average height parents.

*Terminology matters: most people with the condition will not have a problem with being referred to as a person who has achondroplasia; a form of dwarfism; short stature or restricted height. The term 'midget' is an offensive term because of its historical association with 'freak shows'.

*This children's story has focused on the character's name 'Max', any child with the condition wants to be known most importantly by their first name rather than a label.

*For further information visit the understanding dwarfism website: http://www.udprogram.com and other updated links on:
www.strongandmightymax.com

Kristina Gray, Author of 'Strong and Mighty Max'